To ....

From ....

Mr. Men My Brother © 2018 THOIP (a SANRIO company)
Printed and published under licence from Price Stern Sloan, Inc., Los Angeles.
Published in Great Britain by Egmont UK Limited
The Yellow Building, 1 Nicholas Road, London, W11 4AN

ISBN 978 1 4052 8880 4
68175/1
Printed in Italy

MY BROTHER

by Roger Hargreaves

and me

My brother welcomes every day with a smile on his face.

He is full of energy.
He doesn't walk down
the stairs,
he bounces
down
them!

My brother is so funny,
he could even
make
a lion
laugh.

Life is never dull when he is there.

He invents the best games, like a magician.

And tells the best stories, but I'm not always sure if they're true.

He is very brave
and makes impossible things look easy.

But he can get scared, just like me.

He is always surprising me with his tickles.

And he knows just how
to cheer me up when
I'm feeling sad.

My brother loves eating and sometimes his eyes are bigger than his belly.

But his food doesn't always end up in his mouth!

My brother can be as messy as Mr Messy.

And as mischievous as Mr Mischief.

My brother is so much fun to be around.

But he can be a bit grumpy when things don't go his way.

My brother doesn't always do what he's told.

And he sometimes goes
bump when he isn't careful.

My brother
loves animals,
particularly
the noisy,
messy kind.

But he also loves books and would like to be in his own one day - and now he is!

He really is one of a kind.

And he even sleeps in his own unique way.

One day, I think my brother will be famous and drive a sports car.

He would love to swim in a sea of sweets!

He is so cool
and when we're together
the most amazing things happen.

My brother is the greatest
brother ever.

MY BROTHER

My brother is most like **MR.** ....

I love it when my brother plays ....

.... with me.

My brother makes me laugh when ....

....

He is very silly because ....

....

My brother gets into trouble when he ....

....

He is lots of fun and likes ....

Our favourite thing to do together is ....

One day he will be a famous ....

My brother is the greatest because ....

....

This is a picture of my brother:

by ....

aged ....